# INTRODUCING . . .

KU-195-726

Billy

The Giraffe

The
Pelly

The
Duke of
Hampshire

The
Monkey

## Books by Roald Dahl

THE BFG

BILLY AND THE MINPINS

BOY: TALES OF CHILDHOOD

BOY and GOING SOLO

CHARLIE AND THE CHOCOLATE FACTORY

CHARLIE AND THE GREAT GLASS ELEVATOR

THE COMPLETE ADVENTURES OF CHARLIE
AND MR WILLY WONKA

DANNY THE CHAMPION OF THE WORLD

THE ENORMOUS CROCODILE

ESIO TROT

FANTASTIC MR FOX

GEORGE'S MARVELLOUS MEDICINE

THE GIRAFFE AND THE PELLY AND ME

GOING SOLO

JAMES AND THE GIANT PEACH

THE MAGIC FINGER

MATILDA

THE TWITS

THE WITCHES

To discover more books, and find out more about
Roald Dahl, please visit the website at **roalddahl.com**

**Staffordshire Library and Information Services**
Please return or renew by the last date shown

BURTON LIBRARY, HIGH STR
BURTON ON TRENT. TEL. 239
CHILDREN'S LIBRARY

Discard

If not required by other readers, this item may be
renewed in person, by post or telephone, online or by
email. To renew, either the book or ticket are required

**24 Hour Renewal Line**
**0345 33 00 740**

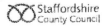

Staffordshire
County Council

STAFFORDSHIRE LIBRARIES

3 8014 09575 178 7

**ROALD DAHL** was a spy, ace fighter pilot, chocolate historian and medical inventor. He was also the author of *Charlie and the Chocolate Factory*, *Matilda*, *The BFG* and many more brilliant stories.

**QUENTIN BLAKE** has illustrated more than three hundred books and was Roald Dahl's favourite illustrator. In 1980 he won the prestigious Kate Greenaway Medal. In 1999 he became the first ever Children's Laureate and in 2013 he was knighted for services to illustration.

# ROALD DAHL

# THE GIRAFFE AND THE PELLY AND ME

Illustrated by **Quentin Blake**

PUFFIN

PUFFIN BOOKS

UK | USA | Canada | Ireland | Australia
India | New Zealand | South Africa

Puffin Books is part of the Penguin Random House group of companies
whose addresses can be found at global.penguinrandomhouse.com.

www.penguin.co.uk   www.puffin.co.uk   www.ladybird.co.uk

Penguin
Random House
UK

First published in the USA by Farrar, Straus and Giroux
and in Great Britain by Jonathan Cape 1985
Reissued by Jonathan Cape with new illustrations 1992
Published by Puffin Books 1993
Reissued 2016
This edition published 2022
001

Text copyright © The Roald Dahl Story Company Ltd, 1985
Illustrations copyright © Quentin Blake, 1992
The moral right of Roald Dahl and Quentin Blake has been asserted

ROALD DAHL is a registered trademark of The Roald Dahl Story Company Ltd
www.roalddahl.com

Printed in Great Britain by Clays Ltd, Elcograf S.p.A.

The authorized representative in the EEA is Penguin Random House Ireland,
Morrison Chambers, 32 Nassau Street, Dublin D02 YH68

A CIP catalogue record for this book is available from the British Library

ISBN: 978-0-241-55850-8

All correspondence to:
Puffin Books, Penguin Random House Children's
One Embassy Gardens, 8 Viaduct Gardens, London SW11 7BW

Words matter. The wonderful words of Roald Dahl can transport you to different worlds
and introduce you to the most marvellous characters. This book was written many years ago,
and so we regularly review the language to ensure that it can continue to be enjoyed by all today.

Puffin Books would like to thank Inclusive Minds for introducing us to its
network of Inclusion Ambassadors. You can read more about the work
Inclusive Minds does here: www.inclusiveminds.com.

MIX
Paper from
responsible sources
FSC
www.fsc.org   FSC® C018179

Penguin Random House is committed to a
sustainable future for our business, our readers
and our planet. This book is made from Forest
Stewardship Council® certified paper.

*For Neisha, Charlotte and Lorina*

Not far from where I live there is a strange old empty wooden house standing all by itself on the side of the road. I long to explore inside it but the door is always locked, and when I peer through a window all I can see is **DARKNESS** and DUST. I know the ground floor used once to be a shop because I can still read the faded lettering across the front which says **THE GRUBBER**. My mother has told me that in our part of the country in the olden days a grubber was another name for a sweet shop, and now every time I look at it I think to myself what a lovely old sweet shop it must have been.

On the shop window itself somebody has painted in white the words **FOR SAIL.**

One morning, I noticed that **FOR SAIL** had been scraped off the shop window and in its place somebody had painted **SOLED.** I stood there staring at the new writing and wishing that it had been me who had bought it because then I would have been able to make it into a grubber all over again. I have always longed and longed to own a sweet shop. The sweet shop of my dreams would be loaded from top to bottom with

# SHERBET SUCKERS

## and CARAMEL FUDGE

and **RUSSIAN TOFFEE**

and **SUGAR SNORTERS**

and **BUTTER GUMBALLS**

and thousands and thousands of other glorious things like that.

Oh boy, what I couldn't have done with that old Grubber shop if it had been mine!

On my next visit to The Grubber, I was standing across the road gazing at the wonderful old building when suddenly an enormous bathtub came sailing out through one of the second-floor windows and

# CRASHED

## RIGHT ON TO THE

## MIDDLE

## OF THE ROAD!

A few moments later, a white porcelain toilet with the wooden seat still on it came flying out of the same window and landed with a wonderful splintering

# CRASH

just beside the bathtub. This was followed by a kitchen sink and an empty canary cage and a four-poster bed and two hot-water bottles and a rocking horse and a sewing machine and goodness knows what else besides.

It looked as though someone was ripping out the whole of the inside of the house with wild abandon, because now pieces of staircase and bits of the banisters and a whole lot of old floorboards came whistling through the windows.

# THEN
# THERE
# WAS
# SILENCE.

I waited and waited but not another sound came
from within the building. I crossed the road and
stood right under the windows and called out,
'Is anybody at home?'

# THERE

# WAS

# NO

# ANSWER.

In the end it began to get dark so I had to turn away and start walking home. But you can bet your life nothing was going to stop me from hurrying back there again tomorrow morning to see what the next surprise was going to be.

When I got back to The Grubber house the next morning, the first thing I noticed was the new door. The dirty old brown door had been taken out and in its place someone had fitted a brand-new red one. The new door was fantastic. It was twice as high as the other one had been and it looked ridiculous. I couldn't begin to imagine who would want a tremendous tall door like that in their house unless it was a **GIANT.**

As well as this, somebody had scraped away the **SOLED** notice on the shop window and now there was a whole lot of different writing all over the glass. I stood there reading it and reading it and trying to figure out what on earth it all meant.

The LWCC Co

THE LADDERLESS
WINDOW-CLEANING
COMPANY ~
Get your windows
cleaned without
a lot of dirty
ladders leaning
against your
house.

I tried to catch some sign or sound of movement inside the house but there was none . . .

## UNTIL ALL OF A **SUDDEN** . . .

## OUT OF THE **CORNER**
### OF MY EYE . . .

I noticed that one of the windows on the top floor

## WAS SLOWLY

## BEGINNING

## TO OPEN

## **OUTWARDS** . . .

Then a **HEAD** appeared at the open window.

I stared at the head. The head stared back at me with big round dark eyes.

Suddenly, a second window was flung wide open and, of all the unexpected things, a

# GIGANTIC

white bird hopped out and perched on the windowsill.

I knew what this one was because of its

amazing beak, which was shaped like a huge orange-coloured basin. **THE PELICAN** looked down at me and sang out:

*'Oh, how I wish*
*For a big fat fish!*
*I'm as hungry as ever could be!*
*A dish of fish is my only wish!*
*How far are we from the sea?'*

'We are a long way from the sea,' I called back to him, 'but there is a fishmonger in the village not far away.'

'A fish *what*?'

'A fish*monger*.'

'Now what on earth would that be?' asked the Pelican. 'I have heard of a fish *pie* and a fish *cake* and a fish *finger*, but I have never heard of a fish*monger*. Are these mongers good to eat?'

This question baffled me a bit, so I said, 'Who is your friend in the next window?'

'She is the **GIRAFFE!**' the Pelican answered. 'Is she not wonderful? Her legs are on the ground floor and her head is looking out of the top window!'

As if all this wasn't enough, the window on the *first floor* was now flung wide open and out popped a **MONKEY!**

The Monkey stood on the windowsill and did a **JIGGLY** little dance. He was so skinny he seemed to be made only out of furry bits of wire, but he danced wonderfully well, and I clapped and cheered and did a little dance myself in return.

'We are the Window Cleaners!' sang out
the Monkey.

*'We will polish your glass*
*Till it's shining like brass*
*And it sparkles like sun on the sea!*
*We are quick and polite,*
*We will come day or night,*
*The Giraffe and the Pelly and me!*

*We're a fabulous crew,*
*We know just what to do,*
*And we never stop work to drink tea.*
*All your windows will glow*

*When we give them a go,*
*The Giraffe and the Pelly and me!*

*We use water and soap*
*Plus some kindness and hope,*
*But we never use ladders, not we.*
*Who needs ladders at all*
*When you're thirty feet tall?*
*Not Giraffe, and not Pelly! Not me!'*

I stood there enthralled. Then I heard the Giraffe saying to the Pelican in the next window, 'Pelly, my dear, be so good as to fly down and bring that small child up here to talk to us.'

At once the Pelican spread his huge white wings and flew down on to the road beside me. 'Hop in,' he said, opening his enormous beak.

I stared at the great orange beak and backed away.

'**GO ON!**' the Monkey shouted from up in his window. 'The Pelly isn't going to *swallow* you! **CLIMB IN!**'

I said to the Pelican, 'I'll only get in if you promise not to shut your beak once I'm inside.'

'**YOU HAVE NOTHING TO FEAR!**' cried the Pelican,

*'And let me tell you why.*
*I have a very special beak!*

*A special beak have I!*
*You'll never see a beak so fine,*
*I don't care where you go.*
*There's magic in this beak of mine!*
*Hop in and don't say no!'*

'I will *not* hop in,' I said, 'unless you swear on your honour you won't shut it once I'm inside. I don't like small dark places.'

'When I have done what I am just about to do,' said the Pelican, 'I won't be *able* to shut it. You don't seem to understand how my beak works.'

'Show me,' I said.

**'WATCH THIS!'** cried the Pelican.

I watched in amazement as the top half of the Pelican's beak began to slide smoothly backwards into his head until the whole thing was almost out of sight.

'It bends and goes down inside the back of my neck!' cried the Pelican. 'Is that not **SENSIBLE?** Is it not **MAGICAL?**'

'It's unbelievable,' I said. 'It's exactly like one of those metal tape measures my parents have at home. When it's out, it's straight. When you slide it back in, it bends and disappears.'

'Precisely,' said the Pelican. 'You see, the top half is of no use to me unless I am chewing fish. The bottom half is what counts, my lad! The bottom half of this glorious beak of mine is the bucket in which we carry our window-cleaning water! So if I didn't slide the top half away I'd be standing around all day long holding it open!

> '*So I slide it away*
> *For the rest of the day!*
> *Even so, I'm still able to speak!*
> *And wherever I've flown*
> *It has always been known*
> *As the Pelican's Patented Beak!*

*If I want to eat fish*
*(That's my favourite dish)*
*All I do is I give it a tweak!*
*In the blink of an eye*
*Out it pops! And they cry,*
*"It's the Pelican's Patented Beak!"* '

# 'STOP SHOWING OFF DOWN THERE!'

shouted the Monkey from the upstairs window.
'Hurry up and bring that small child up to us!
The Giraffe is waiting!'

I climbed into the big
orange beak, and with a
swoosh of wings the Pelican
carried me back to
his perch on the
windowsill.

The Giraffe looked out of her window at me and said, 'How do you do? What is your name?'

'Billy,' I told her.

'Well, Billy,' she said, 'we need your help and we need it fast. We *must have* some windows to clean. We've spent every penny we had on buying this house and we've got to earn some more money quickly.

The Pelly is **STARVING,**
the Monkey is **FAMISHED**
and I am perishing with HUNGER.
The Pelly needs **FISH.**
The Monkey needs **NUTS**
and I am even more difficult to feed. I am a Geraneous Giraffe and a Geraneous Giraffe cannot eat anything except the pink and purple flowers of the **TINKLE-TINKLE TREE.** But those, as I am sure you know, are hard to find and expensive to buy.'

The Pelican cried out, 'Right now I am so hungry I could eat a stale sardine!

'*Has anyone seen a stale sardine*
*Or a bucket of rotten cod?*
*I'd eat the lot upon the spot,*
*I'm such a hungry bod!*'

Every time the Pelican spoke, the beak I was standing in jiggled

# UP

## AND

# DOWN,

and the more excited he got, the more it jiggled.

The Monkey said, 'What Pelly's *really* keen on is salmon!'

'Yes, yes!' cried the Pelican. 'Salmon! Oh, glorious salmon! I dream about it all day long but I never get any!'

'And *I* dream about walnuts!' shouted the Monkey. 'A walnut fresh from the tree is scrumptious-galumptious, so flavoury-savoury, so sweet to eat that it makes me all wobbly just thinking about it!'

At exactly that moment, a huge white Rolls-Royce pulled up right below us, and a chauffeur in a blue and gold uniform got out. He was carrying an envelope in one gloved hand.

'Good heavens!' I whispered. 'That's the Duke of Hampshire's car!'

'Who's he?' asked the Giraffe.

'He's the richest man in England!' I said.

The chauffeur knocked on the door of The Grubber.

He looked up and saw us. He saw the Giraffe, the Pelly, the Monkey and me all staring down at him from above, but not a muscle moved in his face, not an eyebrow was raised. The chauffeurs of very rich people are never surprised by anything they see. The chauffeur said, 'His Grace the Duke of Hampshire has instructed

me to deliver this envelope to The Ladderless
Window-Cleaning Company.'

**'THAT'S US!'** cried the Monkey.

The Giraffe said, 'Be so good as to open the
envelope and read us the letter.'

The chauffeur unfolded the letter and began
to read, '"To whom it may concern, I saw your
notice as I drove by this morning. I have been
looking for a decent window cleaner for the last

fifty years but I have not found one yet. My house has six hundred and seventy-seven windows in it (not counting the greenhouse) and all of them are filthy. Kindly come and see me as soon as possible. Yours truly, Hampshire." That,' added the chauffeur in a voice filled with awe and respect, 'was written by His Grace the Duke of Hampshire in his own hand.'

The Giraffe said to the chauffeur, 'Please tell His Grace the Duke that we will be with him as soon as possible.'

The chauffeur touched his cap and got back into the Rolls-Royce.

# 'WHOOPEE!' shouted

the Monkey.

# 'FANTASTIC!'

cried the Pelican. 'That must be the best window-cleaning job in the world!'

'Billy,' said the Giraffe, 'what is the house called and how do we get there?'

'It is called Hampshire House,' I said. 'It's just over the hill. I'll show you the way.'

'We're off!' cried the Monkey. 'We're off to see the Duke!'

The Giraffe stooped low and went out through the tall door. The Monkey jumped off the windowsill on to the Giraffe's back. The Pelican, with me in his beak hanging on for dear life, flew across and perched on the very top of the Giraffe's head. And away we went.

It wasn't long before we came to the gates of Hampshire House, and as the Giraffe moved slowly up the great wide driveway, we all began to feel just a little bit nervous.

'What's he like, this Duke?' the Giraffe asked me.

'I don't know,' I said. 'But he's very very famous and very rich. People say he has twenty-five gardeners just to look after his flower beds.'

Soon the huge house itself came into view,

# AND

# WHAT

# **A HOUSE**

# IT WAS!

It was like **A PALACE!**

It was **BIGGER** THAN A PALACE!

'Just look at those windows!' cried the Monkey. 'They'll keep us going for ever!'

Then suddenly we heard a man's voice a short

distance away to the right. 'I want those big
black ones at the top of the tree!' the man was
shouting. 'Get me those great big black ones!'

We peered round the bushes and saw an
oldish man with an immense white moustache
standing under a tall cherry tree and pointing

his walking stick in the air. There was a ladder against the tree and another man, who was probably a gardener, was up the ladder.

'Get me those great big black juicy ones right at the very top!' the old man was shouting.

'I can't reach them, Your Grace,' the gardener called back. 'The ladder isn't long enough!'

'Damnation!' shouted the Duke. 'I *was* so looking forward to eating those big ones!'

'Here we go!' the Pelican whispered to me,
and with a **SWISH AND A SWOOP**

he carried me up to the very top of the cherry
tree and there he perched. 'Pick them, Billy!' he
whispered. 'Pick them quickly and put them in
my beak!'

The gardener got such a shock he fell off the
ladder. Down below us, the Duke was shouting,
'My gun! Get me my gun! Some damnable
monster of a bird is stealing my best cherries! Be

off with you, sir! Go away! Those are *my* cherries, not yours! I'll have you shot for this, sir! Where *is* my gun?'

'Hurry, Billy!' whispered the Pelican. 'Hurry, hurry, hurry!'

'My gun!' the Duke was shouting to the gardener. 'Get me my gun, you idiot! I'll have that thieving bird for breakfast, you see if I don't.'

'I've picked them all,' I whispered to the Pelican.

At once the Pelly flew down and landed right beside the furious figure of the Duke of Hampshire, who was prancing about and waving his stick in the air!

'Your cherries, Your Grace!' I said as I leaned over the edge of the Pelican's beak and offered a handful to the Duke.

The Duke was staggered. He reeled back and his eyes POPPED nearly out of their sockets.

'Great Scott!' he gasped. 'Good Lord! What's this?
Who are *you*?'

And now the Giraffe, with the Monkey dancing

about on her back, emerged suddenly from the bushes. The Duke stared at them. He looked as though he was about to burst.

## 'WHO ARE THESE CREATURES?'

he bellowed. 'Has the whole world gone completely daft?'

'We are the Window Cleaners!' sang out the Monkey.

*'We will polish your glass*
*Till it's shining like brass*
*And it sparkles like sun on the sea!*
*We will work for Your Grace*
*Till we're blue in the face,*
*The Giraffe and the Pelly and me!'*

'You *asked* us to come and see you,' the Giraffe said.

The truth was at last beginning to dawn on

the Duke. He put a cherry into his mouth and chewed it slowly. Then he spat out the stone. 'I like the way you picked these cherries for me,' he said. 'Could you also pick my apples in the autumn?'

**'WE COULD!**
 **WE COULD!**
  **OF COURSE WE COULD!'**

we all shouted.

'And who are *you*?' the Duke said, pointing his stick at me.

'He is our Business Manager,' the Giraffe said. 'His name is Billy. We go nowhere without him.'

'Very well, very well,' the Duke muttered. 'Come along with me and let's see if you're any good at cleaning windows.'

I climbed out of the Pelican's beak and the kindly old Duke took me by the hand as we all walked towards the house. When we got there, the Duke said, 'What happens next?'

'It is all very simple, Your Grace,' the Giraffe replied. 'I am the ladder, the Pelly is the bucket and the Monkey is the cleaner. **WATCH US GO!'**

With that, the famous window-cleaning gang sprang into action. The Monkey jumped down from the Giraffe's back and turned on the garden tap. The Pelican held his great beak under the tap until it was full of water.

Then, with a wonderful **SPRINGY LEAP** the Monkey leaped up once again on to the Giraffe's back. From there he scrambled, as easily as if he were climbing a tree, up the long long neck of the Giraffe until he stood balancing on the very top of her head. The Pelican remained standing on the ground beside us, looking up at the Giraffe.

'We'll do the top floor first!' the Giraffe shouted down. 'Bring the water up, please.'

The Duke called out, 'Don't worry about the two top floors. You can't reach them anyway.'

'Who says we can't reach them?' the Giraffe called back.

'I do,' the Duke said firmly, 'and I'm not having any of you risking your silly necks around here.'

If you wish to be friends with a Giraffe, never say anything bad about its neck. Its neck is its proudest possession.

# 'WHAT'S WRONG

# WITH MY NECK?'

snapped the Giraffe.

'Don't argue with me!' cried the Duke. 'If you can't reach it, you can't reach it and that's the end of it! Now get on with your work!'

'Your Grace,' the Giraffe said, giving the Duke a small superior smile, 'there are no windows in the world I cannot reach with this magical neck of mine.'

The Monkey, who was dancing about most dangerously on top of the Giraffe's head, cried out,

'SHOW HIM, GIRAFFEY!

GO ON AND SHOW HIM

WHAT YOU CAN DO WITH YOUR

MAGICAL NECK!'

The next moment, the Giraffe's neck, which heaven knows was long enough already, began to grow longer and **LONGER**

and **LONGER**

and **LONGER**

and **HIGHER**

and **HIGHER**

and **HIGHER**

until at last the Giraffe's head with the Monkey on top of it was level with the windows of the top floor.

The Giraffe looked down from her great height and said to the Duke, 'How's that?'

The Duke was speechless. So was I. It was the

most magical thing I had ever seen, more magical even than the Pelican's Patented Beak.

Up above us, the Giraffe was beginning to sing a little song, but she sang so softly I could hardly catch the words. I think it went something like this:

*'My neck can stretch terribly high,*
*Much higher than eagles can fly.*
*If I ventured to show*
*Just how high it would go*
*You'd lose sight of my head in*
*the sky!'*

The Pelican, with his huge beak full of water, flew up and perched on one of the top-floor windowsills near the Monkey, and now the great window-cleaning business really began.

The speed with which the team worked was

astonishing. As soon as one window was done, the Giraffe moved the Monkey over to the next one and the Pelican followed.

When all the fourth-floor windows on that side of the house were finished, the Giraffe simply drew in her magical neck until the Monkey was level with the third-floor windows and off they went again.

**'AMAZING!'** cried the Duke.

**'ASTONISHING!**
**REMARKABLE!**
**INCREDIBLE!**

I haven't seen out of any of my windows for forty years! Now I shall be able to sit indoors and enjoy the view!'

Suddenly I saw all three of the Window Cleaners stop dead in their tracks. They seemed to freeze against the wall of the house. None of them moved.

'What's happened to them?' the Duke asked me. 'What's gone wrong?'

'I don't know,' I answered.

Then the Giraffe, with the Monkey on her head, tiptoed very gingerly away from the house and came towards us. The Pelican flew with them. The Giraffe came up very close to the Duke and whispered, 'Your Grace, there is a man in one of the bedrooms on the third floor. He is opening all the drawers and taking things out. He's got a pistol!'

The Duke jumped about a foot in the air. 'Which room?' he snapped. 'Show me at once!'

'It's the one on the third floor where the window is wide open,' the Giraffe whispered.

'By gad!' cried the Duke.

## 'THAT'S THE DUCHESS'S BEDROOM!

## HE'S AFTER HER JEWELS!

## CALL THE POLICE!

## SUMMON THE ARMY!

## BRING UP THE CANNON!

## CHARGE WITH THE LIGHT BRIGADE!'

But even as he spoke the Pelican was flying up into the air. As he flew, he turned himself upside down and tipped the window-cleaning water out of his beak. Then I saw the top half of that marvellous patented beak sliding out of his head, ready for action.

'What's that reckless bird up to?' cried the Duke.

'Wait and see,' shouted the Monkey. 'Hold your breath, old man! Hold your nose! Hold your horses and watch the Pelly go!'

Like a bullet the Pelican flew in through the open window, and five seconds later out he came again with his great orange beak firmly closed. He landed on the lawn beside the Duke.

A tremendous **BANGING NOISE**

was coming from inside the Pelican's beak. It sounded as though someone was using a sledgehammer against it from the inside.

'He's got him!' cried the Monkey. 'Pelly's got the burglar in his beak!'

'Well done, sir!' shouted the Duke, hopping about with excitement. Suddenly he pulled the handle of his walking stick upwards, and out of the hollow inside of the stick itself he drew a long thin sharp shining sword. 'I'll run him through!' he shouted, flourishing the sword like a fencer. 'Open up, Pelican! Let me get at him! I'll run the bounder through before he knows what's happened to him! I'll spike him like a pat of butter! I'll feed his gizzards to my foxhounds!'

But the Pelican did not open his beak. He kept it firmly closed and shook his head at the Duke.

The Giraffe shouted, 'The burglar is armed with a pistol, Your Grace! If Pelly lets him out now he'll shoot us all!'

'He can be armed with a *machine gun* for all I care!' bellowed the Duke, his massive moustache bristling like brushwood. 'I'll handle the blighter! Open up, sir! Open up!'

Suddenly there was an **EAR-SPLITTING**

and the Pelican leaped twenty feet into the air. So did the Duke.

'Watch out!' the Duke shouted, taking ten rapid paces backwards. 'He's trying to shoot his way out!' And pointing his sword at the Pelican, he bellowed, 'Keep that beak closed, sir! Don't you dare let him out! He'll murder us all!'

'Shake him up, Pelly!' cried the Giraffe. 'Rattle his bones! Teach him not to do it again!'

The Pelican shook his head so fast from side to side that the beak became a blur and the man inside must have felt he was being scrambled like eggs.

**'WELL DONE, PELLY!'** cried the Giraffe. 'You're doing a great job! Keep on SHAKING him so he doesn't fire that pistol again!'

At this point, a lady with flaming orange hair came flying out of the house shouting,

'MY **JEWELS!**
**SOMEBODY'S**
**STOLEN**
MY JEWELS!

My diamond tiara!

My diamond necklace!

My diamond bracelets!

My diamond earrings!

My diamond rings!

They've had the lot!

My ROOMS have been

**RANSACKED!'**

And then this incredible woman, who fifty-
five years ago had been a world-famous opera
singer, suddenly burst into song.

'My diamonds are over the ocean,

My diamonds are over the sea,

My diamonds were pinched from my bedroom,

Oh, bring back my diamonds to me.'

We were so bowled over by the power of the lady's lungs that all of us, excepting the Pelican, who had to keep his beak closed, joined in the chorus.

*'Bring back, bring back,*
*Oh, bring back my diamonds to me, to me.*
*Bring back, bring back,*
*Oh, bring back my diamonds to me!'*

'Don't worry, Henrietta,' said the Duke. He pointed to the Pelican and said, 'This clever bird, this brilliant burglar-catching creature has saved the day! The bounder's in his beak!'

The Duchess stared at the Pelican. The Pelican stared back at the Duchess and gave her a wink.

'If he's in there,' cried the Duchess, 'why don't you let him out! Then you can run him through with that famous sword of yours! I want my diamonds! Open your beak, bird!'

'No, no!' shouted the Duke. 'He's got a pistol! He'll murder us all!'

Someone must have called the police because

suddenly no less than four squad cars came racing towards us with their sirens screaming.

Within seconds we were surrounded by six police officers, and the Duke was shouting to them, 'The villain you are after is inside the beak of that bird! Stand by to collar him!' And to the Pelican he said,

'GET READY TO **OPEN UP!**

ARE YOU **READY . . .**

**STEADY . . .**

**GO!**

OPEN UP!'

The Pelican opened his gigantic beak and immediately the police officers pounced upon the burglar, who was crouching inside. They snatched his pistol away from him and dragged him out and put handcuffs on his wrists.

'Great Scott!' shouted the Chief of Police. 'It's the Cobra himself!'

'The who! The what!' everyone asked. 'Who's the Cobra?'

'The Cobra is the cleverest and most dangerous cat burglar in the world!' said the Chief of Police.

'He must have climbed up the drainpipe. The Cobra can climb up anything!'

# 'MY **DIAMONDS!**'

## DEMANDED THE DUCHESS.

## 'I WANT MY **DIAMONDS!**

## WHERE ARE MY **DIAMONDS?'**

**'HERE THEY ARE!'** cried the Chief
of Police, fishing great handfuls of jewellery
from the burglar's pockets.

The Duchess was overcome with relief.

When the police had taken away the fearsome burglar known as the Cobra, and the Duchess had returned to the house, the old Duke stood on the lawn with the Giraffe, the Pelican, the Monkey and me.

'Look!' cried the Monkey. 'That rotten burglar's bullet has made a hole in poor Pelly's beak!'

'That's done it,' said the Pelican. 'Now it won't be any use for holding water when we clean the windows.'

'Don't you worry about that, my dear Pelly,' said the Duke, patting him on the beak. 'My chauffeur will soon put a patch over it the same way he mends the tyres on the Rolls. Right now we have far more important things to talk about than a little hole in a beak.'

We stood there waiting to see what the Duke was going to say next.

'Now listen to me, all of you,' he said. 'Those diamonds were worth millions! Millions and millions! And *you* have saved them!'

## THE MONKEY NODDED.

## THE GIRAFFE SMILED.

## THE PELICAN BLUSHED.

'No reward is too great for you,' the Duke went on. 'I am therefore going to make you an offer which I hope will give you pleasure. I hereby invite the Giraffe and the Pelican and the Monkey to live on my estate for the rest of their lives.

'I shall give you my best and largest hay barn as your private house. Central heating, showers, a kitchen and anything else you desire for your comfort will be installed.

'In return, you will keep my windows clean, and pick my cherries and my apples. If the Pelican is willing, perhaps he will also give me a ride in his beak now and again.'

'A pleasure, Your Grace!' cried the Pelican. 'Would you like a ride now?'

'Later,' said the Duke. 'I'll have one after tea.'

At this point, the Giraffe gave a nervous little cough and looked up at the sky.

'Is there a problem?' asked the Duke. 'If there is, do please let me hear it.'

'I don't like to sound ungrateful or pushy,' murmured the Giraffe, 'but we do have one very pressing problem. We are all absolutely famished. We haven't eaten for days.'

'My *dear* Giraffey!' cried the Duke. 'How very thoughtless of me. Food is no problem around here.'

'I'm afraid it is not quite as easy as all that,' said the Giraffe. 'You see, I myself happen to be –'

'Don't tell me!' cried the Duke. 'I know it already! I am an expert on the animals of Africa. The moment I saw you I knew you were no ordinary giraffe. You are of the Geraneous variety, are you not?'

'You are absolutely right, Your Grace,' said the Giraffe. 'But the trouble with us is that we only eat –'

'You don't have to tell me that either!' cried the Duke. 'I know perfectly well a Geraneous Giraffe can eat only one kind of food. Am I not right in thinking that the pink and purple flowers of the **TINKLE-TINKLE TREE** are your only diet?'

'Yes,' sighed the Giraffe, 'and that's been my problem ever since I arrived on these shores.'

'That is no problem at all here at Hampshire House,' said the Duke. 'Look over there, my dear Giraffey, and you will see the only plantation of **TINKLE-TINKLE TREES** in the entire country!'

The Giraffe looked. She gave a gasp of astonishment, and at first she was so overwhelmed she couldn't even speak. Great tears of joy began running down her cheeks.

'Help yourself,' said the Duke. 'Eat all you want.'

'Oh, my sainted souls!' gasped the Giraffe. 'Oh, my naked neck!

# I CANNOT
# **BELIEVE**
# WHAT I AM SEEING!'

The next moment she was galloping full speed across the lawns and whinnying with excitement and the last we saw of her, she was burying her head in the beautiful pink and purple flowers that blossomed on the tops of the trees all around her.

'As for the Monkey,' the Duke went on, 'I think he also will be pleased with what I have to offer. All over my estate there are thousands of giant nut trees . . .'

'Nuts?' cried the Monkey. 'What kind of nuts?'

'Walnuts, of course,' said the Duke.

'Walnuts!' screamed the Monkey.

'Not walnuts? You don't really mean walnuts?

# YOU'RE PULLING MY LEG!

# YOU'RE JOKING!

# YOU CAN'T BE SERIOUS!

# I MUST HAVE HEARD **WRONG!'**

'There's a walnut tree right over there,' the Duke said, pointing.

The Monkey took off like an arrow, and a few seconds later he was high up in the branches of the walnut tree, cracking the nuts and guzzling what was inside.

'That leaves only the Pelly,' said the Duke.

'Yes,' said the Pelican nervously, 'but I'm afraid that what I eat does not grow on trees. I only eat fish. Would it be too much trouble, I wonder, if I were to ask you for a reasonably fresh piece of haddock or cod every day?'

'Haddock or cod!' shouted the Duke, spitting out the words as though they made a bad taste in his mouth. 'Cast your eyes, my dear Pelly, over there to the south.'

The Pelican looked across the vast rolling estate and in the distance he saw a great river.

'That is the River Hamp!' cried the Duke. 'The finest salmon river in the whole of Europe!'

# 'SALMON!'

## SCREECHED THE PELICAN.

## 'NOT **SALMON?**

## YOU DON'T REALLY MEAN **SALMON?'**

'It's *full* of salmon,' the Duke said, 'and I own it. You can help yourself.'

Before he had finished speaking the Pelican was in the air. The Duke and I watched him as he flew full speed towards the river. We saw him circle over the water, then he dived and disappeared. A few moments later, he was in the air again, and he had a **GIGANTIC** salmon in his beak.

I stood alone with the Duke on the lawn beside his great house. 'Well, Billy,' he said, 'I'm glad they are all happy. But what about you, my lad? I am wondering if you happen to have just one extra special little wish all for yourself. If you do, I'd love you to tell me about it.'

## THERE WAS A SUDDEN
# TINGLING IN MY TOES.

It felt as though
# SOMETHING TREMENDOUS
might be going to happen

to me any moment.

'Yes,' I murmured nervously. 'I do have one extra special little wish.'

'And what might that be?' said the Duke in a kindly voice.

'There is an old wooden house near where I live,' I said. 'It's called The Grubber and long ago it used to be a sweet shop. I have wished and wished that one day somebody might come along and make it into a marvellous new sweet shop all over again.'

'Somebody?' cried the Duke. 'What do you mean, *somebody*? You and I will do that! We'll do

it together! We'll make it into the most wonderful
sweet shop in the world! And *you*, my boy, will
own it!'

Whenever the old Duke got excited, his

enormous moustache started to bristle and jump about. Right now it was jumping up and down so much it looked as though he had a squirrel on his face. 'By Gad, sir!' he cried, waving his stick, 'I shall buy the place today! Then we'll get to work and have the whole thing ready in no time! You just wait and see what sort of a sweet shop we are going to make out of this Grubber place of yours!'

It was amazing how quickly things began to happen after that. There was no problem about buying the house because it was owned by the Giraffe and the Pelly and the Monkey, and they insisted upon giving it to the Duke for nothing.

Then builders and carpenters moved in and rebuilt the whole of the inside so that once again

it had three floors. On all these floors they put
together rows and rows of tall shelves, and there
were ladders to climb up to the highest shelves
and baskets to carry what you bought.

Then the sweets and chocs and toffees and fudges and nougats began pouring in to fill the shelves. They came by aeroplane from every country in the world, the most wild and wondrous things you could ever imagine.

There were **GUMTWIZZLERS**
and **FIZZWINKLES** from China,

FROTHBLOWERS and
SPITSIZZLERS from Africa,

**TUMMYTICKLERS** and
**GOBWANGLES** from the Fiji Islands

and **LIPLICKERS**
and **PLUSHNUGGETS** from
the Land of the Midnight Sun.

For two whole weeks the flood of boxes and
sacks continued to arrive. I could no longer keep
track of all the countries they came from, but you
can bet your life that as I unpacked each new batch

I sampled it carefully. I can remember especially
the **GIANT WANGDOODLES** from
Australia, every one with a huge ripe red straw-
berry hidden inside its crispy chocolate crust . . .

and the **ELECTRIC FIZZCOCKLERS** that made every hair on your head stand straight up on end as soon as you popped one into your mouth . . .

and there were **NISHNOBBLERS**
and **GUMGLOTTERS**
and **BLUE BUBBLERS**
and **SHERBET SLURPERS**
and **TONGUE RAKERS,**

and as well as all this, there was a whole lot of splendid stuff from the great Wonka factory itself, for example the famous **WILLY WONKA RAINBOW DROPS** – suck them and you can spit in six different colours.

And his **STICKJAW** for talkative parents.

And his **MINT JUJUBES** that will give the child next door green teeth for a month.

On the Grand Opening Day, I decided to allow all my customers to help themselves for free, and the place was so crowded with children you could hardly move. The television cameras and the newspaper reporters were all there, and the old Duke himself stood outside in the road

with my friends the Giraffe and the Pelly and the Monkey watching the marvellous scene. I came out of the shop to join them for a few moments and I brought each of them a bag of extra-special sweets as a present.

To the Duke, because the weather was a little chilly, I gave some

# SCARLET SCORCHDROPPERS

that had been sent to me from Iceland. The label said that they were guaranteed to make the person who sucked them as warm as toast even if he were standing stark naked at the North Pole in mid-winter. The moment the Duke popped one into his mouth, thick smoke came gushing out of the old boy's nostrils in such quantities that I thought his moustache was going up in flames.

# 'TERRIFIC!' he cried, hopping

about. 'Tremendous stuff! I'll take a case of them home with me!'

To the Giraffe I gave a bag of

# GLUMPTIOUS GLOBGOBBLERS.

The Globgobbler is an especially delicious sweet that is made somewhere near Marrakech, and the moment you bite into it, all the perfumed juices of Morocco go squirting down your gullet one after the other.

'It's wonderful!' cried the Giraffe as a cascade of lovely liquid flavours poured all the way down her long long throat. 'It's even better than my favourite pink and purple flowers!'

To the Pelican I gave a big bag of

# PISHLETS.

Pishlets, as you probably know, are bought by children who are unable to whistle a tune as they walk along the street but long to do so. They had a splendid effect upon the Pelican, for after he had put one of them into his beak and chewed it for a while, he suddenly started singing like a nightingale. This made him wildly excited because Pelicans are not song-birds. No Pelican had ever been known to whistle a tune before.

To the Monkey I gave a bag of

# DEVIL'S DRENCHERS,

those small fiery black sweets that one is not
allowed to sell to children under four years old.
When you have sucked a Devil's Drencher for a
minute or so, you can set your breath alight and
blow a huge column of fire twenty feet into the
air. The Duke put a match to the Monkey's breath
and shouted, 'Blow, Monkey, blow!' A sheet of
orange flame shot up as high as the roof of the
Grubber house and it was wonderful.

'I've got to leave you now,' I said. 'I must go
and look after my customers in the shop.'

'We must go, too,' said the Giraffe. 'We have
one hundred windows to clean before dark.'

I said goodbye to the Duke, and then one by
one I said goodbye to the three best friends I had
ever had. Suddenly, we all became very quiet and

melancholy, and the Monkey looked as though he was about to cry as he sang me a little song of farewell:

*'We have tears in our eyes*
*As we wave our goodbyes,*
*We so loved being with you, we three.*
*So do please now and then*
*Come and see us again,*
*The Giraffe and the Pelly and me.*
*All you do is to look*
*At a page in this book*
*Because that's where we always will be.*
*No book ever ends*
*When it's full of your friends*
*The Giraffe and the Pelly and me.'*

# LET'S FIND OUT
## HOW **CAREFULLY** YOU
## WERE READING . . .

**1.** WHAT WAS THE WORD FOR A SWEET SHOP IN THE OLDEN DAYS?

a. A flubber

b. A grubber

c. A tucker

**2.** WHAT COLOUR IS THE NEW DOOR OF THE SHOP?

a. Blue

b. Green

c. Red

**3.** WHAT JOB DO THE PELICAN, GIRAFFE AND MONKEY DO?

a. Window cleaners

b. Plumbers

c. Electricians

**4.** WHAT KIND OF TREE DOES THE GIRAFFE'S FAVOURITE FOOD COME FROM?

a. The Umpty-Numpty tree

b. The Tinkle-Tinkle tree

c. The Lovely-Jubbly tree

**5.** HOW MANY YEARS HAS IT BEEN SINCE THE DUKE HAS BEEN ABLE TO SEE OUT OF HIS DIRTY WINDOWS?

a. 100

b. 3

c. 40

ANSWERS: 1. b 2. c 3. a 4. b 5. c

Are you ready for another adventure? Then turn the page to meet the **BIG FRIENDLY GIANT . . .**

**THE BFG**

## CHAPTER ONE
# THE WITCHING HOUR

Sophie couldn't sleep.

A brilliant moonbeam was slanting through a gap in the curtains. It was shining right on to her pillow.

The other children in the dormitory had been asleep for hours.

Sophie closed her eyes and lay quite still. She tried very hard to doze off.

It was no good. The moonbeam was like a silver blade **SLICING** through the room on to her face.

## THE HOUSE WAS ABSOLUTELY SILENT.

No voices came up from downstairs. There were no footsteps on the floor above either.

The window behind the curtain was wide open, but nobody was walking on the pavement outside. No cars went by on the street. Not the tiniest sound could be heard anywhere. Sophie had never known such a

# SILENCE.

Perhaps, she told herself, this was what they called the witching hour.

The witching hour, somebody had once whispered to her, was a special moment in the middle of the night when every child and every grown-up was in a deep deep sleep, and all the dark things came out from hiding and had the world to themselves.

The moonbeam was brighter than ever on Sophie's pillow. She decided to get out of bed and close the gap in the curtains.

You got punished if you were caught out of bed after lights-out. Even if you said you had to go to the lavatory, that was not accepted as an excuse and they punished you just the same. But there was no one about now, Sophie was sure of that.

She reached out for her glasses that lay on the chair beside her bed. They had steel rims and very thick lenses, and she could hardly see a thing without them. She put them on, then she slipped out of bed and tiptoed over to the window.

When she reached the curtains, Sophie hesitated. She longed to duck underneath them and lean out of the window to see what the world looked like now that the witching hour was at hand.

She listened again. Everywhere it was

# DEATHLY STILL.

The longing to look out became so strong she couldn't resist it. Quickly, she ducked under the curtains and leaned out of the window.

In the silvery moonlight, the village street she knew so well seemed completely different. The houses looked bent and crooked, like houses in a fairy tale. Everything was pale and ghostly and milky-white.

Across the road, she could see Mrs Rance's shop, where you bought buttons and wool and bits of elastic. It didn't look real. There was something dim and misty about that too.

Sophie allowed her eye to travel further and further down the street.

# SUDDENLY SHE FROZE.

THERE WAS SOMETHING

COMING UP THE STREET ON

THE OPPOSITE SIDE.

IT WAS SOMETHING

**DARK . . .**

SOMETHING **TALL**

AND **DARK . . .**

SOMETHING VERY

# TALL

AND VERY

## DARK

AND VERY

# THIN.

## CHAPTER TWO
# WHO?

It wasn't a human. It couldn't be. It was four times as tall as the tallest human. It was so tall its head was higher than the upstairs windows of the houses. Sophie opened her mouth to scream, but no sound came out. Her throat, like her whole body, was frozen with fright.

This was the witching hour all right.

The tall dark figure was coming her way. It was keeping very close to the houses across the street, hiding in the shadowy places where there was no moonlight.

On and on it came, nearer and nearer. But it was moving in spurts. It would stop, then it would move on, then it would stop again.

But what on earth was it doing?

**AH-HA!** Sophie could see now what it was up to. It was stopping in front of each house. It would stop and peer into the upstairs window of each house in the street. It actually had to bend down to peer into the upstairs windows. That's how tall it was.

It would stop and peer in. Then it would slide on to the next house and stop again, and peer in, and so on all along the street.

It was much closer now and Sophie could see it more clearly.

Looking at it carefully, she decided it *had* to be some kind of PERSON. Obviously it was not a human. But it was definitely a PERSON.

A GIANT PERSON, perhaps.

Sophie stared hard across the misty moonlit street. The Giant (if that was what he was) was wearing a long BLACK CLOAK.

In one hand he was holding what looked like a VERY LONG, THIN TRUMPET.

In the other hand, he held a LARGE SUITCASE.

The Giant had stopped now right in front of Mr and Mrs Goochey's house. The Goocheys had a greengrocer's shop in the middle of the High Street, and the family lived above the shop. The two Goochey children slept in the upstairs front room, Sophie knew that.

The Giant was peering through the window into the room where Michael and Jane Goochey were sleeping. From across the street, Sophie watched and held her breath.

She saw the Giant step back a pace and put the suitcase down on the pavement. He bent over and opened the suitcase. He took something out of it. It looked like a glass jar, one of those square ones with a screw top. He unscrewed the top of the jar and poured what was in it into the end of the long trumpet thing.

Sophie watched, **TREMBLING.**

She saw the Giant straighten up again and she saw him poke the trumpet in through the open upstairs window of the room where the Goochey children were sleeping. She saw the Giant take a deep breath and

**WHOOF,**

he blew through the trumpet.

No noise came out, but it was obvious to Sophie that whatever had been in the jar had now been blown through the trumpet into the Goochey children's bedroom.

What could it be?

As the Giant withdrew the trumpet from the window and bent down to pick up the suitcase he happened to turn his head and glance across the street.

In the moonlight, Sophie caught a glimpse of an enormous long wrinkly face with the most enormous ears. The nose was as sharp as a knife, and above the nose there were two bright flashing eyes, and the eyes were staring straight at Sophie. There was a **FIERCE** and **DEVILISH** look about them.

Sophie gave a yelp and pulled back from the window. She flew across the dormitory and jumped into her bed and hid under the blanket.

And there she crouched, still as a mouse, and tingling all over.

# ROALD DAHL STORY DAY

**13 SEPTEMBER**

EVERY SEPTEMBER, together with our fans across the world, we **CELEBRATE** our FAVOURITE **ROALD DAHL STORIES,** CHARACTERS and WORLDS!

FIND OUT MORE AT
**www.roalddahl.com**

That's it.
The end of the book.

HERE IS
**one** LAST **WORD,**
**invented** by **Roald Dahl** HIMSELF.
**Make sure you KEEP IT SAFE.**

# HIPSWITCH

**Adverb:** Doing something very quickly.

# ROALD
# DAHL